Book 7

CIRQUE DU FREAK
THE SAGA OF DARREN SHAN

*Hunters of
the Dusk*

Book 7

Cirque Du Freak

The Saga of Darren Shan

Hunters of the Dusk

by Darren Shan

 LITTLE, BROWN AND COMPANY

New York ⋅ Boston

Copyright © 2002 by Darren Shan
Cover art copyright © 2005 by Rick Raymond

Little, Brown and Company

Hachette Book Group USA
237 Park Avenue, New York, NY 10017
Visit our Web site at www.lb-teens.com

First U.S. Mass Market Edition: September 2005

The characters and events portrayed in this book are fictitious.
Any similarity to real persons, living or dead, is coincidental and not
intended by the author

First published in Great Britain by Collins in 2002.

Library of Congress Cataloging-in-Publication Data

Shan, Darren.
    Hunters of the dusk / by Darren Shan. — 1st U.S. ed.
        p.   cm. (The saga of Darren Shan ; bk. 7)
    Sequel to: The Vampire Prince.
    Summary: Darren Shan leaves Vampire Mountain as part of an
elite force on a life-and-death mission to find the newly-risen
Vampaneze Lord, who is set to lead the vampaneze into war
against the vampires.
ISBN 978-0-316-00098-7 (mm)
    [1. Vampires — Fiction.   2. Horror Stories.]   I. Title: At head
of title: Cirque Du Freak. II. Title
PZ7.S52823 Hu 2004
[Fic] — dc22

10   9   8   7   6   5

Q-BF

Printed in the United States of America

For:

Shirley & Derek — "Beauty and the Beast"

Sparring partners:
Gillie Russell & Zoë Clarke

Ringside crew:
The Christopher Little Clan

OBEs (Order of the Bloody Entrails) to:
Kerri "Carve Yer Guts Up" Goddard-Kinch
"La Femme Fatale" Christine Colinet

Also in the **CIRQUE DU FREAK** series:

PROLOGUE

IT WAS AN AGE of tragic mistakes. For me, the tragedy began fourteen years earlier when, mesmerized by a vampire's amazing performing tarantula, I stole it from him. After an initially successful theft, everything went to hell, and I paid for my crime with my humanity. Faking my own death, I left my family and home, and traveled the world with the Cirque Du Freak, as the assistant to a blood-drinking creature of the night.

My name's Darren Shan. I'm a half-vampire.

I'm also — through a series of events so astounding I still have trouble believing they really happened — a Vampire Prince. The Princes are the leaders of the vampire clan, respected and obeyed by all. There are only five of them — the others are Paris Skyle, Mika Ver Leth, Arrow, and Vancha March.

I'd been a Prince for six years, living within the

Halls of Vampire Mountain (the stronghold of the clan), learning the customs and traditions of my people, and how to be a vampire of good standing. I'd also been learning the ways of warfare, and how to use weapons. The rules of battle were essential to any vampire's education, but now more than ever — because we were at war.

Our opponents were the vampaneze, our purple-skinned blood-cousins. They're a lot like vampires in many ways, except in one key area — they kill whenever they drink blood. Vampires don't harm those they feed from — we simply take a small amount of blood from each human we target — but vampaneze believe it's shameful to feed without draining their victims dry.

Though there was no love lost between the vampires and vampaneze, for hundreds of years an uneasy truce had existed between the two clans. That changed six years ago when a group of vampaneze — aided by a vampire traitor called Kurda Smahlt — stormed Vampire Mountain in an attempt to seize control of the Hall of Princes. We defeated them (thanks largely to my discovery of the plot prior to their assault), then interrogated the survivors, baffled by why they should choose to attack.

Unlike vampires, vampaneze had no leaders —

they were entirely democratic — but when they split from the vampires six hundred years ago, a mysterious, powerful magician known as Mr. Tiny paid them a visit and placed the Coffin of Fire in their possession. This coffin burned alive anyone who lay within it — but Mr. Tiny said that one night a man would lie down in it and step out unharmed, and that man would lead them into a victorious war with the vampires, establishing the vampaneze as the unopposed rulers of the night.

During the interrogation, we learned to our horror that the Lord of the Vampaneze had finally arisen, and vampaneze across the world were preparing for the violent, bloody war to come.

Once our assailants had been put to a painful death, word spread from Vampire Mountain like wildfire: "We're at war with the vampaneze!" And we'd been locked in combat with them ever since, fighting grimly, desperate to disprove Mr. Tiny's dark prophecy — that we were destined to lose the war and be wiped from the face of the earth . . .

CHAPTER ONE

IT WAS ANOTHER LONG, tiring night in the Hall of Princes. A Vampire General called Staffen Irve was reporting to me and Paris Skyle. Paris was the oldest living vampire, with more than eight hundred years under his belt. He had flowing white hair, a long, grey beard, and had lost his right ear in a fight many decades ago.

Staffen Irve had been active in the field for three years, and had been giving us a quick rundown of his experiences in the War of the Scars, as it had come to be known (a reference to the scars on our fingertips, the common mark of a vampire or vampaneze). It was a strange war. There were no big battles and neither side used missile-firing weapons — vampires and vampaneze fight only with hand-to-hand weapons like swords, clubs, and spears. The war was a series of

e or four vampires at a time
ber of vampaneze, fighting to the

four of us 'gainst three of them,"
Staffen Irve said, telling us about one of his more recent encounters. "But my lads was dry behind the tonsils, while the vampaneze was battle-hardy. I killed one of 'em but the others got away, leaving two of my lads dead and the third with a useless arm."

"Have any of the vampaneze spoke of their Lord?" Paris asked.

"No, sire. Those I take alive only laugh at my questions, even under torture."

In the six years that we'd been hunting for their Lord, there'd been no sign of him. We knew he hadn't been blooded — various vampaneze had told us that he was learning their ways before becoming one of them — and the general opinion was that if we were to have any chance of preventing Mr. Tiny's predictions, we had to find and kill their Lord before he took full control of the clan.

A cluster of Generals was waiting to speak with Paris. They moved forward as Staffen Irve departed, but I signaled them back. Picking up a mug of warm blood, I passed it to the one-eared Prince. He smiled and drank deeply, then wiped red stains from around his mouth with the back of a trembling hand — the responsibility of running the war council was taking its toll on the ancient vampire.

"Do you want to call it a night?" I asked, worried about Paris's health.

He shook his head. "The night is young," he muttered.

"But you are not," said a familiar voice behind me — Mr. Crepsley. The vampire in the red cloak spent most of his time by my side, advising and encouraging me. He was in a peculiar position. As an ordinary vampire, he held no recognizable rank, and could be commanded by the lowliest of Generals. Yet as my guardian he unofficially had the powers of a Prince (since I followed his advice practically all the time). In reality, Mr. Crepsley was second in command to Paris Skyle, yet nobody openly acknowledged this. Vampire protocol — go figure!

"You should rest," Mr. Crepsley said to Paris, laying a hand on the Prince's shoulder. "This war will run a long time. You must not exhaust yourself too early. We will need you later."

"Nonsense!" Paris laughed. "You and Darren are the future. I am the past, Larten. I will not live to see the end of this war if it drags on as long as we fear. If I do not make my mark now, I never will."

Mr. Crepsley started to object, but Paris silenced him with the crooking of a finger. "An old owl hates to be told how young and virile he is. I am on my last legs, and anyone who says otherwise is a fool, a liar, or both."

Mr. Crepsley tilted his head obediently. "Very well. I will not argue with you."

Paris sniffed. "I should hope not," he said, then shifted tiredly on his throne. "But this *has* been a taxing night. I will talk with these Generals, then crawl off to my coffin to sleep. Will Darren be able to manage without me?"

"Darren will manage," Mr. Crepsley said confidently, and stood slightly behind me as the Generals advanced, ready to advise when required.

Paris didn't make his coffin by dawn. The Generals had much to argue about — by studying reports on the movements of the vampaneze, they were trying to pinpoint the possible hiding place of their Lord — and it was close to midday before the ancient Prince slipped away.

I treated myself to a short break, grabbed some food, then heard from three of the Mountain's fighting tutors, who were training the latest batch of Generals. After that I had to send two new Generals out into the field for their first taste of combat. I quickly went through the small ceremony — I had to daub their foreheads with vampire blood and mutter an ancient war prayer over them — then wished them luck and sent them off to kill vampaneze — or die.

Then it was time for vampires to approach me with a wide range of problems and questions. As a Prince I was expected to deal with every sort of subject under the moon. I was only a young, inexperienced half-vampire, who'd become a Prince more by default than merit, but the members of the clan placed their trust completely in their Princes, and I was given the same respect as Paris or any of the others.

When the last vampire had departed, I snagged about three hours of sleep, in a hammock that I'd strung up at the rear of the Hall. When I woke, I ate some half-cooked, salted boar meat, washed down with water and followed by a small mug of blood. Then it was back to my throne for more planning, plotting, and reports.

CHAPTER TWO

I SNAPPED OUT OF SLEEP to the sound of screaming.

Jerking awake, I fell out of my hammock, onto the hard, cold floor of my rocky cell. My hand automatically felt for the short sword that I kept strapped by my side at all times. Then the fog of sleep cleared and I realized it was only Harkat, having a nightmare.

Harkat Mulds was a Little Person, a short creature who wore blue robes and worked for Mr. Tiny. He'd been human once, though he didn't remember who he used to be, or when or where he lived. When he died, his soul remained trapped on Earth, until Mr. Tiny brought him back to life in a new, stunted body.

"Harkat," I mumbled, shaking him roughly. "Wake up. You're dreaming again."

Harkat had no eyelids, but his large green eyes dimmed when he was asleep. Now the light in them flared and he moaned loudly, rolling out of his hammock, as I had moments before. "Dragons!" he screamed, voice muffled by the mask he always wore — he wasn't able to breathe normal air for more than ten or twelve hours, and without the mask he'd die. "Dragons!"

"No," I sighed. "You've been dreaming."

Harkat stared at me with his unnatural green eyes, then relaxed and tugged his mask down, revealing a wide, grey, jagged gash of a mouth. "Sorry, Darren. Did I wake . . . you?"

"No," I lied. "I was up already."

I swung back onto my hammock and sat gazing at Harkat. There was no denying he was an ugly creature. Short and squat, with dead, grey skin, no visible ears or a nose — he had ears stitched beneath the skin of his scalp, but was without a sense of smell or taste. He had no hair, round, green eyes, sharp little teeth, and a dark grey tongue. His face had been stitched together, like Frankenstein's monster.

Of course, I was no model myself — few vampires were! My face, body, and limbs were laced with scars and burn marks, many picked up during my Trials of Initiation (which I'd passed at my second attempt, two years ago). I was also as bald as a baby, as a result of my first set of Trials, when I'd been badly burnt.

Harkat was one of my closest friends. He'd saved my life twice, when I was attacked by a wild bear on the trail to Vampire Mountain, then in a fight with savage boars during my first, failed Trials of Initiation. It bothered me to see him so disturbed by the nightmares that had been plaguing him for the last few years.

"Was this nightmare the same as the others?" I asked.

"Yes." He nodded. "I was wandering in a vast wasteland. The sky was red. I was searching for something but I didn't . . . know what. There were pits full of stakes. A dragon attacked. I fought it off but . . . another appeared. Then another. Then . . ." He sighed miserably.

Harkat's speech had improved greatly since he'd first started speaking. In the beginning he'd had to pause for breath after every two or three words, but he'd learned to control his breathing and now only stalled during long sentences.

"Were the shadow men there?" I asked. Sometimes he dreamed of shadowy figures who chased and tormented him.

"Not this time," he said, "though I think they'd have appeared if you . . . hadn't woken me up." Harkat was sweating — his sweat was a pale green color —

13

and his shoulders shook slightly. He suffered greatly in his sleep, and stayed awake as long as he could, sleeping only four or five hours out of every seventy-two.

"Want something to eat or drink?" I asked.

"No," he said. "Not hungry." He stood and stretched his burly arms. He was wearing only a cloth around his waist, so I could see his smooth stomach and chest — Harkat had no nipples or belly button.

"It's good to see you," he said, pulling on his blue robes, which he'd never grown out of the habit of wearing. "It's been ages since . . . we got together."

"I know," I groaned. "This war business is killing me, but I can't leave Paris to deal with it alone. He needs me."

"How is Sire Skyle?" Harkat asked.

"Bearing up. But it's hard. So many decisions to make, so many troops to organize, so many vampires to send to their deaths."

We were silent a while, thinking about the War of the Scars and the vampires — including some very good friends of ours — who had died in it.

"How've you been?" I asked Harkat, shrugging off the morbid thoughts.

"Busy," he said. "Seba's working me harder all the time." After a few months of milling around Vampire Mountain, Harkat had gone to work for the quartermaster, Seba Nile, who was in charge of stocking and maintaining the Mountain's stores of food, clothes, and weapons. Harkat started out moving crates and sacks around, but he'd learned quickly about supplies and how to keep up with the needs of the vampires, and now served as Seba's senior assistant.

"Do you have to return to the Hall of Princes soon?" Harkat asked. "Seba would like to see you. He wants to show you . . . some spiders." The mountain was home to thousands of arachnids, known as Ba'Halen's spiders.

"I have to go back," I said regretfully, "but I'll try to drop by soon."

"Do," Harkat said seriously. "You look exhausted. Paris is not the only one who . . . needs rest."

Harkat had to leave shortly afterward to prepare for the arrival of a group of Generals. I lay in my hammock and stared at the dark rock ceiling, unable to get back to sleep. This was the cell Harkat and I had first shared when we came to Vampire Mountain. I liked this tiny cubbyhole — it was the closest thing I had to a bedroom — but rarely got to see much of it. Most of my nights were spent in the Hall of Princes, and the few free hours I had by day were normally passed eating or exercising.

I ran a hand over my bald head while I was resting

and thought back over my Trials of Initiation. I'd sailed through them the second time. I didn't have to take them — as a Prince, I was under no obligation — but I wouldn't have felt right if I hadn't. By passing the Trials, I'd proved myself worthy of being a vampire.

Apart from the scars and burns, I hadn't changed much in the last six years. As a half-vampire, I aged only one year for every five that passed. I was a little taller than when I left the Cirque Du Freak with Mr. Crepsley, and my features had thickened and matured slightly. But I wasn't a full-vampire and wouldn't change much until I became one. As a full-vampire I'd be much stronger. I'd also be able to heal cuts with my spit, breathe out a gas that could knock people unconscious, and communicate telepathically with other vampires. Plus I'd be able to flit, which is a super-fast speed vampires can attain. On the downside, I'd be vulnerable to sunlight and couldn't move around during the day.

But all that lay far ahead. Mr. Crepsley hadn't said anything about when I'd be fully blooded, but I gathered it wouldn't happen until I was an adult. That was ten or fifteen years away — my body was still that of a teenager — so I had lots of time to enjoy (or endure) my extended childhood.

I lay relaxing for another half hour, then got up

and dressed. I'd taken to wearing light blue clothes, pants and a tunic, covered by a long, regal-looking robe. My right thumb snagged on the arm of the tunic as I was pulling it on, as it often did — I'd broken the thumb six years ago and it still stuck out at an awkward angle.

Taking care not to rip the fabric on my extra-tough nails — which could gouge holes in soft rock — I freed my thumb and finished dressing. I pulled on a pair of light shoes and ran a hand over my head to make sure I hadn't been bitten by ticks. They'd appeared all over the mountain recently, annoying everyone. Then I made my way back to the Hall of Princes for another long night of tactics and debate.

CHAPTER THREE

THE DOORS TO THE HALL of Princes could be opened only by a Prince laying a hand on the doors or touching a panel on the thrones inside the Hall. Nothing could break through the walls of the Hall, which had been built by Mr. Tiny and his Little People centuries before.

The Stone of Blood was kept in the Hall, and was very important. It was a magical artifact. Any vampire who came to the mountain (most of the three thousand vampires in the world had made the trek at least once) laid their hands on the Stone and let it absorb some of their blood. The Stone could then be used to track that vampire down. So, if Mr. Crepsley wanted to know where Arrow was, he could lay his hands on the Stone and think about him, and within seconds he'd have a fix on the Prince. Or, if he thought of an area, the Stone would tell him how many vampires were there.

I couldn't use the Stone of Blood to search for others — only full-vampires were able to do that — but I could be traced through it, since it had taken blood from me when I became a Prince.

If the Stone ever fell into the hands of the vampaneze, they could use it to track down all the vampires who'd bonded with it. Hiding from them would be impossible. They'd annihilate us. Because of this danger, some vampires wanted to destroy the Stone of Blood — but there was a legend that it could save us in our hour of greatest need.

I was thinking about all this while Paris used the Stone of Blood to maneuver troops in the field. As reports reached us of vampaneze positions, Paris used the Stone to check where his Generals were, then communicated telepathically with them, giving them orders to move from place to place. It was this that drained him so deeply. Others could have used the Stone, but as a Prince, Paris's word was law, and it was quicker for him to deliver the orders himself.

While Paris focused on the Stone, Mr. Crepsley and me put field reports together and built up a clear picture of the movements of the vampaneze. Many other

Generals were also doing this, but it was our job to take their findings, sort through them, pick out the more important ones, and make suggestions to Paris. We had lots of maps, with pins marking the positions of vampires and vampaneze.

Mr. Crepsley had been intently studying a map for ten minutes, and he looked worried. "Have you seen this?" he asked eventually, calling me over.

I stared at the map. There were three yellow flags and two red flags stuck close together around a city. We used five main colors to keep track of things. Blue flags for vampires. Yellow for vampaneze. Green for vampaneze strongholds — cities and towns that they defended like bases. White flags were stuck in places where we'd won fights. Red flags where we'd lost.

"What am I looking for?" I asked, staring at the yellow and red flags. My eyes were bleary from lack of sleep and too much concentrating on maps and poorly scrawled reports.

"The name of the city," Mr. Crepsley said, running a fingernail over it.

The name meant nothing to me at first. Then my head cleared. "That's your original home," I muttered. It was the city where Mr. Crepsley had lived when he was human. Twelve years ago, he'd returned, taking me and Evra Von — a snake-boy from the Cirque Du Freak — with him, to stop a crazy vampaneze called Murlough, who'd gone on a killing spree.

"Find the reports," Mr. Crepsley said. There was a number on each flag, linking it to reports in our files, so we knew exactly what each flag represented. After a few minutes, I found the relevant sheets of paper and quickly scanned them.

"Of the vampaneze seen there," I muttered, "two were heading into the city. The other was leaving. The first red flag's from a year ago — four Generals were killed in a large clash with several vampaneze."

"And the second red flag marks the spot where Staffen Irve lost two of his men," Mr. Crepsley said. "It was when I was adding this flag to the map that I noticed the degree of activity around the city."

"Do you think it means anything?" I asked. It was unusual for so many vampaneze to be sighted in one location.

"I am not sure," he said. "The vampaneze may have made a base there, but I do not see why — it is out of the way of their other strongholds."

"We could send someone to check," I suggested.

He considered that, then shook his head. "We have already lost too many Generals there. It is not a strategically important site. Best to leave it alone."

Mr. Crepsley rubbed the long scar that divided the flesh on the left side of his face and went on staring at the map. He'd cut his orange crop of hair tighter than usual — most vampires were cutting their hair short, because of the ticks — and he looked almost bald in the strong light of the Hall.

"It bothers you, doesn't it?" I noted.

He nodded. "If they *have* set up a base, they must be feeding on the humans. I still consider it home, and I do not like to think of my spiritual neighbors and relations suffering at the hands of the vampaneze."

"We could send in a team to get rid of them."

He sighed. "That would not be fitting. I would be putting personal considerations before the welfare of the clan. If I ever get out in the field, I shall check on the situation myself, but there is no need to send others."

"What are the chances of you and me ever getting out of here?" I asked. I didn't enjoy fighting, but after six years cooped up inside the mountain, I'd have given my fingernails for a few nights out in the open, even if it meant taking on a dozen vampaneze single-handed.

"The way things stand — poor," Mr. Crepsley admitted. "I think we will be stuck here until the end of the war. If one of the other Princes suffers a serious injury and withdraws from battle, we might have to replace him. Otherwise . . ." He drummed his fingers on the map and grimaced.

"*You* don't have to stay," I said quietly. "There are plenty of others who could guide me."

He barked a laugh. "There are plenty who would steer you," he agreed, "but how many would clip you around the ear if you made an error?"

"Not many," I said, chuckling.

"They think of you as a Prince," he said, "whereas I still think of you first and foremost as a meddlesome little brat with a *penchant* for stealing spiders."

"Charming!" I huffed. I knew he was kidding — Mr. Crepsley always treated me with the respect my position deserved — but there was some truth to his teasing. There was a special bond between Mr. Crepsley and me, like between a father and son. He could say things to me that no other vampire would dare. I'd be lost without him.

Placing the map of Mr. Crepsley's former home to one side, we returned to the more important business of the night, little dreaming of the events that would eventually lead us back to the city of Mr. Crepsley's youth and the awful confrontation with evil that awaited us there.

CHAPTER FOUR

THE HALLS AND TUNNELS of Vampire Mountain were buzzing with excitement — Mika Ver Leth had returned after an absence of five years, and the rumor was that he had news of the Vampaneze Lord! I was in my cell, resting, when word came. Wasting no time, I pulled on my clothes and hurried to the Hall of Princes at the top of the mountain, to check if the stories were true.

Mika was talking with Paris and Mr. Crepsley when I arrived, surrounded by a pack of Generals eager for news. He was dressed entirely in black, as was his custom, and his hawklike eyes seemed darker and grimmer than ever. He raised one gloved hand in salute when he saw me pushing my way forward. I stood to attention and saluted back. "How's the cub Prince?" he asked with a quick, tight grin.

"Not bad," I replied, studying him for signs of injury — many who returned to Vampire Mountain carried the scars of battle. But although Mika looked tired, he hadn't been visibly wounded. "What about the Vampaneze Lord?" I asked directly. "According to the gossip, you know where he is."

Mika grimaced. "If only!" Looking around, he said, "Shall we assemble? I *have* news, but I'd rather announce it to the Hall in general." Everyone present made straight for their seats. Mika settled on his throne and sighed contentedly. "It's good to be back," he said, patting the arms of the hard chair. "Has Seba been taking good care of my coffin?"

"To the vampaneze with your coffin!" a General shouted, momentarily forgetting his place. "What news of the Vampaneze Lord?"

Mika ran a hand through his jet-black hair. "First, let's make it clear — I don't know where he is." A groan spread through the Hall. "But I've had word of him," Mika added, and all ears pricked up.

"Before I begin," Mika said, "do you know about the latest vampaneze recruits?" Everybody looked blank. "The vampaneze have been adding to their ranks since the start of the war, blooding more humans than usual, to drive their numbers up."

"This is old news," Paris murmured. "There are

far fewer vampaneze than vampires in the world. We expected them to blood recklessly. It is nothing to worry about — we still outnumber them greatly."

"Yes," Mika said. "But now they're also using unblooded humans. They call them 'vampets.' Apparently the Vampaneze Lord himself came up with the name. Like him, they're learning the rules of vampaneze life and warfare as humans, before being blooded. He plans to build an army of human helpers."

"We can deal with humans," a General snarled, and there were shouts of agreement.

"Normally," Mika agreed. "But we must be wary of these vampets. While they lack the powers of the vampaneze, they're learning to fight like them. Also, since they aren't blooded, they don't have to abide by the more restrictive vampaneze laws. They aren't honor-bound to tell the truth, they don't have to follow ancient customs — and they don't have to limit themselves to hand-to-hand weapons."

Angry mutters swept through the Hall.

"The vampaneze are using *guns?*" Paris asked, shocked. The vampaneze were even stricter than vampires where weapons were involved. We could use boomerangs and spears, but most vampaneze wouldn't touch them.

"The vampets aren't vampaneze," Mika said with

a grunt. "There's no reason why a non-blooded vampet shouldn't use a gun. I don't think all their masters approve, but under orders from their Lord, they allow it.

"But the vampets are a problem for another night," Mika continued. "I only mention them now because it's relevant to how I found out about their Lord. A vampaneze would die screaming before betraying his clan, but the vampets aren't so hardened. I captured one a few months ago and squeezed some interesting details out of him. First — the Vampaneze Lord doesn't have a base. He's traveling the world with a small band of guards, moving among the various fighting units, keeping up morale."

The Generals received the news with great excitement — if the Vampaneze Lord was mobile and lightly protected, he was more vulnerable to attack.

"Did this *vampet* know where the Vampaneze Lord was?" Mr. Crepsley asked.

"No," Mika said. "He'd seen him, but that had been more than a year ago. Only those who accompany him know of his travel patterns."

"What else did he tell you?" Paris inquired.

"That their Lord still hasn't been blooded. And that despite his efforts, morale is low. Vampaneze losses are high, and many don't believe they can win the war. There has been talk of a peace treaty — even outright surrender."

Loud cheering broke out. Some Generals were so elated by Mika's words that a group swept forward, picked him up, and carried him from the Hall. They could be heard singing and shouting as they headed for the crates of ale and wine stored below. The other, more sober Generals looked to Paris for guidance.

"Go on," the elderly Prince smiled. "It would be impolite to let Mika and his overeager companions drink alone."

The remaining Generals applauded the announcement and hurried away, leaving only a few Hall attendants, myself, Mr. Crepsley, and Paris behind.

"This is foolish," Mr. Crepsley grumbled. "If the vampaneze are truly considering surrender, we should push hard after them, not waste time —"

"Larten," Paris interrupted. "Follow the others, find the largest barrel of ale you can, and get good and steaming drunk."

Mr. Crepsley stared at the Prince, his mouth wide open. "Paris!" he gasped.

"You have been caged in here too long," Paris said. "Go and unwind, and do not return without a hangover."

"But —" Mr. Crepsley began.

"That is an order, Larten," Paris growled.

Mr. Crepsley looked as though he'd swallowed a live eel, but he was never one to disobey an order from a superior, so he clicked his heels together, muttered, "Aye, sire," and stormed off to the storerooms in a huff.

"I've never seen Mr. Crepsley with a hangover," I said, laughing. "What's he like?"

"Like a . . . what do the humans say? A gorilla with a sore head?" Paris coughed into a fist — he'd been coughing a lot lately — then smiled. "But it will do him good. Larten takes life too seriously sometimes."

"What about you?" I asked. "Do you want to go?"

Paris pulled a sour face. "A mug of ale would prove the end of me. I shall take advantage of the break by lying in my coffin at the back of the Hall and getting a full day's sleep."

"Are you sure? I can stay if you want."

"No. Go and enjoy yourself. I will be fine."

"OK." I hopped off my throne and made for the door.

"Darren," Paris said, calling me back. "An excessive amount of alcohol is as bad for the young as for the old. If you are wise, you will drink in moderation."

"Remember what you told me about wisdom a few years ago, Paris?" I replied.

"What?"

"You said the only way to get wise was to get experienced." Winking, I rushed out of the Hall and was soon sharing a barrel of ale with a grumpy, orange-haired vampire. Mr. Crepsley gradually cheered up as the night progressed, and was singing loudly by the time he reeled back to his coffin late the following morning.

CHAPTER FIVE

I COULDN'T UNDERSTAND WHY there were two moons in the sky when I awoke, or why they were green. Groaning, I rubbed the back of a hand over my eyes, then looked again. I realized I was lying on the floor, staring up at the green eyes of a chuckling Harkat Mulds. "Have fun last night?" he asked.

"I've been poisoned," I moaned, rolling over onto my stomach, feeling as though I was on the deck of a ship during a fierce storm.

"You won't be wanting boar guts and . . . bat broth then?"

"Don't!" I winced, weak at the very thought of food.

"You and the others must have drained . . . half the mountain's supply of ale last night," Harkat remarked, helping me to my feet.

"Is there an earthquake?" I asked as he let go of me.

"No," he said, puzzled.

"Then why's the floor shaking?"

He laughed and steered me to my hammock. I'd been sleeping inside the door of our cell. I had vague memories of falling off the hammock every time I tried to get on. "I'll just sit on the floor a while," I said.

"As you wish." Harkat chortled. "Would you like some ale?"

"Go away or I'll hit you," I growled.

"Is ale no longer to your liking?"

"No!"

"That's funny. You were singing about how much you . . . loved it earlier. 'Ale, ale, I drink like a whale, I am the . . . Prince, the Prince of ale.'"

"I could have you tortured," I warned him.

"Never mind," Harkat said. "The whole clan went crazy . . . last night. It takes a lot to get a vampire drunk, but . . . most managed. I've seen some wandering the tunnels, looking like —"

"Please," I begged, "don't describe them." Harkat laughed again, pulled me to my feet, and led me out of the cell into the maze of tunnels. "Where are we going?" I asked.

"The Hall of Perta Vin Grahl. I asked Seba about

cures . . . for hangovers — I had a feeling you'd have one — and he said . . . a shower usually did the trick."

"No!" I moaned. "Not the showers! Have mercy!"

Harkat took no notice of my pleas, and soon he was shoving me under the icy cold waters of the internal waterfalls in the Hall of Perta Vin Grahl. I thought my head was going to explode when the water first struck, but after a few minutes the worst of my headache had passed and my stomach had settled. By the time I was toweling myself dry, I felt a hundred times better.

We passed a green-faced Mr. Crepsley on our way back to our cell. I bid him a good evening, but he only snarled in reply.

"I'll never understand the appeal of . . . alcohol," Harkat said as I was dressing.

"Haven't you ever gotten drunk?" I replied.

"Perhaps in my past life, but not since . . . becoming a Little Person. I don't have taste buds, and alcohol doesn't . . . affect me."

"Lucky you," I muttered sourly.

Once I'd dressed, we strolled up to the Hall of Princes to see if Paris needed me, but it was largely deserted and Paris was still in his coffin.

"Let's go on a tour of the tunnels . . . beneath the

Halls," Harkat suggested. We'd done a lot of exploring when we first came to the mountain, but it had been two or three years since we'd last gone off on an adventure.

"Don't you have work to do?" I asked.

"Yes, but . . ." He frowned. It took a while to get used to Harkat's expressions — it was hard to know whether someone without eyelids and a nose was frowning or grinning — but I'd learned to read them. "It will hold. I feel strange. I need to be on the move."

"OK," I said. "Let's go walk around."

We started in the Hall of Corza Jarn, where trainee Generals were taught how to fight. I'd spent many hours here, mastering the use of swords, knives, axes, and spears. Most of the weapons were designed for adults, and were too large for me to master, but I'd picked up the basics.

The highest-ranking tutor was a blind vampire called Vanez Blane. He'd been my Trials Master during both my Trials of Initiation. He'd lost his left eye in a fight with a lion many decades before, and lost the second six years ago in a fight with the vampaneze.

Vanez was wrestling with three young Generals. Though he was blind, he'd lost none of his sharpness, and the trio quickly ended up flat on their backs at the hands of the ginger-haired games master. "You'll have to learn to do better than that," he told them. Then, with his back to us, he said, "Hello, Darren. Greetings, Harkat Mulds."

"Hi, Vanez," we replied, not surprised that he knew who we were — vampires have very keen senses of smell and hearing.

"I heard you singing last night, Darren," Vanez said, leaving his three students to recover and regroup.

"No!" I gasped, crestfallen. I'd thought Harkat was joking about that.

"Very enlightening," Vanez said with a smile.

"I didn't!" I groaned. "Tell me I didn't!"

Vanez's smile spread. "I shouldn't worry. Plenty of others made asses of themselves, too."

"Ale should be banned," I growled.

"Nothing wrong with ale," Vanez disagreed. "It's the ale-*drinkers* who need to be controlled."

We told Vanez we were going on a tour of the lower tunnels and asked if he'd like to come. "Not much point," he said. "I can't see anything. Besides . . ." Lowering his voice, he told us the three Generals he was training were due to be sent into action soon. "Between ourselves, they're as poor a trio as I've ever passed." He sighed. Many vampires were being rushed into the field, to replace casualties in the War of the Scars. It was a point of disagreement among the clan — it usually took a minimum of twenty years to be declared a General of good standing — but Paris said that desperate times called for desperate measures.

Leaving Vanez, we made for the storerooms to see Mr. Crepsley's old mentor, Seba Nile. At seven hundred, Seba was the second-oldest vampire. He dressed in red like Mr. Crepsley and spoke in the same precise way. He was wrinkled and shrunken with age, and limped badly — like Harkat — from a wound to his left leg gained in the same fight that had claimed Vanez's eye.

Seba was delighted to see us. When he heard we were going exploring, he insisted on coming with us. "There is something I wish to show you," he said.

As we left the Halls and entered the vast warren of lower connecting tunnels, I scratched my bald head with my fingernails.

"Ticks?" Seba asked.

"No," I said. "My head's been itching like mad lately. My arms and legs too, and my armpits. I think I have an allergy."

"Allergies are rare among vampires," Seba said. "Let me examine you." Luminous lichen grew along many of the walls and he was able to study me by the light of a thick patch. "Hmmm." He smiled briefly, then released me.

"What is it?" I asked.

"You are coming of age, Master Shan."

"What does that have to do with itching?"

"You will find out," he said mysteriously.

Seba kept stopping at webs to check on spiders. The old quartermaster was strangely fond of the eight-legged predators. He didn't keep them as pets, but he spent a lot of time studying their habits. He was able to communicate with them using his thoughts. Mr. Crepsley could too, and so could I.

"Ah!" he said eventually, stopping at a large cobweb. "Here we are." Putting his lips together, he whistled softly, and moments later a big grey spider with strange green spots scuttled down the cobweb and onto Seba's upturned hand.

"Where did that come from?" I asked, stepping forward for a closer look. It was larger than the normal mountain spiders, and different in color.

"Do you like it?" Seba asked. "I call them Ba'Shan's spiders. I hope you do not object — the name seemed appropriate."

"Ba'Shan's spiders?" I repeated. "Why would —"

I stopped. Fourteen years ago, I'd stolen a poisonous spider from Mr. Crepsley — Madam Octa. Eight years later, I'd released her — on Seba's advice — to make a new home with the mountain spiders. Seba said she wouldn't be able to mate with the others. I hadn't seen her since I set her free, and had almost forgotten about her. But now the memory snapped into place, and I knew where this new spider had come from.

"It's one of Madam Octa's, isn't it?" I groaned.

"Yes," Seba said. "She mated with Ba'Halen's spiders. I noticed this new strain three years ago, although it is only this last year that they have multiplied. They are taking over. I think they will become the dominant mountain spider, perhaps within ten or fifteen years."

"Seba!" I snapped. "I only released Madam Octa because you told me she couldn't have offspring. Are they poisonous?"

The quartermaster shrugged. "Yes, but not as deadly as their mother. If four or five attacked together, they could kill, but not one by itself."

"What if they go on a rampage?" I yelled.

"They will not," Seba said stiffly.

"How do you know?"

"I have asked them not to. They are incredibly intelligent, like Madame Octa. They have almost the same mental abilities as rats. I am thinking of training them."

"To do *what?*" I said, laughing.

"Fight," he said darkly. "Imagine if we could send armies of trained spiders out into the world, with orders to find vampaneze and kill them."

I turned appealingly to Harkat. "Tell him he's crazy. Make him see sense."

Harkat smiled. "It sounds like a good idea . . . to me," he said.

"Ridiculous!" I snorted. "I'll tell Mika. He hates spiders. He'll send troops down here to stamp them out."

"Please do not," Seba said quietly. "Even if they cannot be trained, I enjoy watching them develop. Please do not rid me of one of my few remaining pleasures."

I sighed and cast my eyes to the ceiling. "OK. I won't tell Mika."

"Nor the others," he pressed. "I would be highly unpopular if word leaked."

"What do you mean?"

Seba cleared his throat guiltily. "The ticks," he muttered. "The new spiders have been feeding on ticks, so they have moved upward to escape."

"Oh," I said, thinking of all the vampires who'd had to cut their hair and beards and shave under their arms because of the deluge of ticks. I grinned.

"Eventually the spiders will pursue the ticks to the top of the mountain and the epidemic will pass," Seba continued, "but until then I would rather nobody knew what was causing it."

I laughed. "You'd be strung up if this got out!"

"I know," he said with a grimace.

I promised to keep word of the spiders to myself. Then Seba headed back for the Halls — the short trip had tired him — and Harkat and I continued down the tunnels. The farther we progressed, the quieter Harkat got. He seemed uneasy, but when I asked him what was wrong, he said he didn't know.

Eventually we found a tunnel that led outside. We followed it to where it opened onto the steep mountain face, and sat staring up at the evening sky. It had been months since I'd been out in the open, and more than two years since I'd slept outside. The air tasted fresh and welcome, but strange.

"It's cold," I noted, rubbing my hands up and down my bare arms.

"Is it?" Harkat asked. His dead grey skin registered only extreme degrees of heat or cold.

"It must be late autumn or early winter." It was hard keeping track of the seasons when you lived inside a mountain.

Harkat wasn't listening. He was scanning the

forests and valleys below, as if he expected to find someone there.

I walked a short bit down the mountain. Harkat followed, then overtook me and picked up speed. "Careful," I called, but he paid no attention. Soon he was running, and I was left behind, wondering what he was playing at. "Harkat!" I yelled. "You'll trip and crack your skull if you —"

I stopped. He hadn't heard a word. Cursing, I slipped off my shoes, flexed my toes, and then started after him. I tried to control my speed, but that was impossible on such a steep slope, and soon I was racing down the mountain, sending pebbles and dust scattering, yelling with excitement and terror.

Somehow we stayed on our feet and reached the bottom of the mountain in one piece. Harkat kept running until he came to a small circle of trees, where he finally stopped and stood as though frozen. I jogged after him. "What . . . was that . . . about?" I gasped.

Raising his left hand, Harkat pointed toward the trees.

"What?" I asked, seeing nothing but trunks, branches, and leaves.

"He's coming," Harkat hissed.

"Who?"

"The dragon master."

I stared at Harkat. He looked as though he was awake, but perhaps he'd dozed off and was sleepwalking. "I think we should get you back inside," I said, taking his outstretched arm. "We'll find a fire and —"

"Hello, boys!" somebody yelled from within the circle of trees. "Are you the welcoming committee?"

Letting go of Harkat's arm, I stood beside him — now as stiff as he was — and stared again into the cluster of trees. I thought I recognized that voice — though I hoped I was wrong!

Moments later, three figures emerged from the gloom. Two were Little People, who looked almost exactly like Harkat, except they had their hoods up and moved with a stiffness that Harkat had worked out of his system during his years among the vampires. The third was a small, smiling, white-haired man, who struck more fear in me than a band of invading vampaneze.

Mr. Tiny!

After more than six hundred years, Desmond Tiny had returned to Vampire Mountain, and I knew as he strode toward us, beaming, like a rat catcher in league with the Pied Piper of Hamlin, that his reappearance meant nothing but trouble.

CHAPTER SIX

MR. TINY PAUSED when he reached us. The short, plump man was wearing a shabby yellow suit — a thin jacket, no overcoat — with childish-looking green rain boots and a chunky pair of glasses. The heart-shaped watch he always carried hung by a chain from the front of his jacket. Some said Mr. Tiny was an agent of fate — his first name was Desmond, and if you shortened it and put the two names together, you got *Mr. Destiny*.

"You've grown, young Shan," he said, running an eye over me. "And you, Harkat . . ." He smiled at the Little Person, whose green eyes seemed wider and rounder than ever. "*You* have changed beyond recognition. Wearing your hood down, working for vampires — and talking!"

"You knew . . . I could talk," Harkat muttered,

slipping back into his old broken speech habits. "You always . . . knew."

Mr. Tiny nodded, then started forward. "Enough of the chitchat, boys. I have work to do and I must be quick. Time is precious. A volcano's due to erupt on a small tropical island tomorrow. Everybody within a ten-mile radius will be roasted alive. I want to be there — it sounds like great fun."

He wasn't joking. That's why everyone feared him — he took pleasure in tragedies that left anyone halfway human shaken to their very core.

We followed Mr. Tiny up the mountain, trailed by the two Little People. Harkat looked back often at his "brothers." I think he was communicating with them — the Little People can read each other's thoughts — but he said nothing to me about it.

Mr. Tiny entered the mountain by a different tunnel from the one we'd used. It was a tunnel I'd never been in, higher, wider, and drier than most. There were no twists or side tunnels leading off it. It rose straight up the spine of the mountain. Mr. Tiny saw me staring at the walls of the unfamiliar tunnel. "This is one of my shortcuts," he said. "I've shortcuts all over the world, in places you wouldn't dream of. Saves time."

As we progressed, we passed groups of very pale-skinned humans in rags, lining the sides of the tunnel, bowing low to Mr. Tiny. These were the Guardians of the Blood, people who lived within Vampire Mountain and donated their blood to the vampires. In return, they were allowed to extract a vampire's internal organs and brain when he died — which they ate at special ceremonies!

I felt nervous walking past the ranks of Guardians — I'd never seen so many of them gathered together before — but Mr. Tiny only smiled and waved at them, and didn't stop to talk.

Within a quarter of an hour we were at the gate that opened onto the Halls of Vampire Mountain. The guard on duty swung the door wide open when we knocked but stopped when he saw Mr. Tiny and half closed it again. "Who are you?" he snapped defensively, hand snaking to the sword on his belt.

"You know who I am, Perlat Cheil," Mr. Tiny said, brushing past the startled guard.

"How do you know my — ?" Perlat Cheil began, then stopped and gazed after the departing figure. He was trembling, and his hand had fallen away from his sword. "Is that who I think it is?" he asked as I passed with Harkat and the Little People.

"Yes," I said simply.

"Charna's guts!" he gasped, and made the death's touch sign by pressing the middle finger of his right hand to his forehead, and the two fingers next to that over his eyelids. It was a sign vampires made when they thought death was close.

Through the tunnels we marched, silencing conversations and causing jaws to drop. Even those who'd never met Mr. Tiny recognized him, stopped what they were doing and fell in behind us, following wordlessly, as though part of a funeral procession.

There was only one tunnel leading to the Hall of Princes — I'd found another six years ago, but that had since been blocked off — and it was protected by the Mountain's finest guards. They were supposed to stop and search anyone seeking entry to the Hall, but when Mr. Tiny approached, they gawked at him, lowered their weapons, then let him — and the rest of the procession — pass.

Mr. Tiny finally stopped at the doors of the Hall and glanced at the domed building that he'd built six centuries earlier. "It's stood the test of time quite well, hasn't it?" he remarked to no one in particular. Then, laying a hand on the doors, he opened them and entered. Only Princes were supposed to be able to open the doors, but it didn't surprise me that Mr. Tiny had the power to control them too.

Mika and Paris were within the Hall, discussing the war with a group of Generals. There were a lot of sore heads and bleary eyes, but everyone snapped to attention when they saw Mr. Tiny striding in.

"By the teeth of the gods!" Paris gasped, his face whitening. He cringed as Mr. Tiny set foot on the platform of thrones, then drew himself straight and forced a tight smile. "Desmond," he said, "it is good to see you."

"You too, Paris," Mr. Tiny responded.

"To what do we owe this unexpected pleasure?" Paris asked with strained politeness.

"Wait a minute and I'll tell you," Mr. Tiny replied, then sat down on a throne — *mine!* — crossed his legs, and made himself comfortable. "Get the gang in," he said, crooking a finger at Mika. "I've something to say and it's for everybody's ears."

Within a few minutes, almost every vampire in the mountain had crowded into the Hall of Princes and stood nervously by the walls — as far away from Mr. Tiny as possible — waiting for the mysterious visitor to speak.

Mr. Tiny had been checking his nails and rubbing them up and down the front of his jacket. The Little People were standing behind the throne. Harkat stood to their left, looking uncertain. I sensed he didn't know whether to stand with his brothers-of-nature or with his brothers-of-choice — the vampires.

"All present and correct?" Mr. Tiny asked. He got to his feet and waddled to the front of the platform. "Then I'll come straight to the point. The Lord of the Vampaneze has been blooded." He paused, anticipating gasps, groans, and cries of terror. But we all just stared at him, too shocked to react. "Six hundred years ago," he continued, "I told your forebears that the Vampaneze Lord would lead the vampaneze into a war against you and wipe you out. That was *a* truth — but not *the* truth. The future is both open and closed. There's only one 'will be' but there are often hundreds of 'can be's.' Which means the Vampaneze Lord and his followers *can* be defeated."

Breath caught in every vampire's throat and you could feel hope forming in the air around us, like a cloud.

"The Vampaneze Lord is only a half-vampaneze at the moment," Mr. Tiny said. "If you find and kill him before he's fully blooded, victory will be yours."

At that, a huge roar went up, and suddenly vampires were clapping each other on the back and cheering. A few didn't join in the hooting and hollering. Those with firsthand knowledge of Mr. Tiny — myself, Paris, Mr. Crepsley — sensed he hadn't finished, and guessed there must be a catch. Mr. Tiny wasn't the kind to smile broadly when delivering good news. He grinned like that only when he knew there was going to be suffering and misery.

When the wave of excitement had died down, Mr. Tiny raised his right hand. He clutched his heart-shaped watch with his left hand. The watch glowed a dark red color, and suddenly his right hand glowed as well. All eyes settled on the five crimson fingers and the Hall went eerily quiet.

"When the Vampaneze Lord was discovered seven years ago," Mr. Tiny said, his face illuminated by the glow of his fingers, "I studied the strings connecting the present to the future, and saw that there were five chances to avert the course of destiny. One of those has already come and gone."

The red glow faded from his thumb, which he tucked down into his palm. "That chance was Kurda Smahlt," he said. Kurda was the vampire who had led the vampaneze against us, in a bid to seize control of the Stone of Blood. "If Kurda had succeeded, most vampires would have joined the vampaneze and the War of the Scars — as you call it — would have been prevented.

"But you killed him, destroying what was probably your best hope of survival in the process." He shook his head. "That was silly."

"Kurda Smahlt was a traitor," Mika growled.

"Nothing good comes of treachery. I'd rather die honorably than owe my life to a traitor."

"More fool you," Mr. Tiny said with a laugh, then wiggled his glowing little finger. "This represents your last chance, if all others fail. It will not fall for some time yet — if at all — so we shall ignore it." He tucked the glowing finger down, leaving the three middle fingers standing.

"Which brings us to my reason for coming. If I left you to your own devices, these chances would slip by unnoticed. You'd carry on as you have been, the opportunities would pass, and before you knew it . . ." He made a soft popping sound.

"Within the next twelve months," he said softly but clearly, "there may be three encounters between certain vampires and the Vampaneze Lord — assuming you heed my advice. Three times he will be at your mercy. If you seize one of these chances and kill him, the war will be yours. If you fail, there'll be one final, all-deciding confrontation, upon which the fate of every living vampire will hang." He paused teasingly. "To be honest, I hope it goes down to the wire — I love big, dramatic conclusions!"

He turned his back on the Hall and one of his Little People handed him a flask, from which he drank deeply. Furious whispers and conversations swept through the assembled vampires while he was drinking, and when he next faced the crowd, Paris Skyle was waiting. "You have been very generous with your information, Desmond," he said. "On behalf of all here, I thank you."

"Don't mention it," Mr. Tiny said. His fingers had stopped glowing, he'd let go of his watch, and his hands now rested in his lap.

"Will you extend your generosity and tell us which vampires are destined to encounter the Vampaneze Lord?" Paris asked.

"I will," Mr. Tiny said smugly. "But let me make one thing clear — the encounters will occur only if the vampires *choose* to hunt the Lord of the Vampaneze. The three I name don't have to accept the challenge of hunting him down, or take responsibility for the future of the vampire clan. But if they don't, you're doomed, for in these three alone lies the ability to change that which is destined to be."

He slowly looked around the Hall, meeting the eyes of every vampire present, searching for signs of weakness and fear. Not one of us looked away or wilted in the face of such a dire charge. He grunted. "Very well," he said. "One of the hunters is absent, so I'll not name him. If the other two head for the cave of Lady Evanna, they'll probably run into him along the way. If not, his chance to play an active part in the future will pass, and it will boil down to that lone pair."

"And they are . . . ?" Paris asked tensely.

Mr. Tiny glanced over at me, and with a horrible sinking feeling in my gut, I guessed what was coming next. "The hunters must be Larten Crepsley and his assistant, Darren Shan," Mr. Tiny said simply, and as all eyes in the Hall turned to us, I had the sense of invisible tumblers clicking into place, and knew my years of quiet security inside Vampire Mountain had come to an end.

CHAPTER SEVEN

THE POSSIBILITY OF REFUSING the challenge never entered my thoughts. Six years of living among vampires had filled me with their values and beliefs. Any vampire would lay down his life for the good of the clan. Of course, this wasn't as simple as giving one's life — I had a mission to fulfill, and if I failed, all would suffer — but the principle was the same. I'd been chosen, and a vampire who's chosen does not say "no."

There was a short debate, in which Paris told Mr. Crepsley and me that this was not official duty and we didn't have to agree to represent the clan — no shame would befall us if we refused to cooperate with Mr. Tiny. At the end of the debate, Mr. Crepsley stepped forward, red cloak snapping behind him like wings, and said, "I relish the chance to hunt down the Vampaneze Lord."

I stepped up after him, sorry I wasn't wearing my impressive blue cloak, and said in what I hoped was a brave tone, "Me too."

"The boy knows how to keep it short," Mr. Tiny murmured, winking at Harkat.

"What about the rest of us?" Mika asked. "I've spent five years hunting for that accursed Lord. I wish to accompany them."

"Aye! Me too!" a General in the crowd shouted, and soon everyone was bellowing at Mr. Tiny, seeking permission to join us in the hunt.

Mr. Tiny shook his head. "Three hunters must seek — no more, no less. Non-vampires may assist them, but if any of their kinsmen tag along, they shall fail."

Angry mutters greeted that statement.

"Why should we believe you?" Mika asked. "Surely ten stand a better chance than three, and twenty more than ten, and thirty —"

Mr. Tiny snapped his fingers. There was a loud, sharp sound and dust fell from overhead. Looking up, I saw long jagged cracks appear in the ceiling of the Hall of Princes. Other vampires saw them too and cried out, alarmed.

"Would you, who has not seen three centuries, dare to tell me, who measures time in continental drifts, about the mechanisms of fate?" Mr. Tiny asked menacingly. He snapped his fingers again and the cracks spread. Chunks of the ceiling crumbled inward. "A thousand vampaneze couldn't chip the walls of this Hall, yet I, by snapping my fingers, can bring it tumbling down." He lifted his fingers to snap them again.

"No!" Mika shouted. "I apologize! I didn't mean to offend you!"

Mr. Tiny lowered his hand. "Think of this before crossing me again, Mika Ver Leth," he growled, then nodded at the Little People he'd brought with him, who headed for the doors of the Hall. "They'll patch the roof up before we leave," Mr. Tiny said. "But next time you anger me, I'll reduce this Hall to rubble, leaving you and your precious Stone of Blood to the whim of the vampaneze."

Blowing dust off his heart-shaped watch, Mr. Tiny smiled around the Hall again. "I take it we're decided — three it shall be?"

"Three," Paris agreed.

"Three," Mika muttered bleakly.

"As I said, non-vampires may — indeed, *must* — play a part, but for the next year no vampire should seek out any of the hunters, unless for reasons that have nothing to do with the search for the Vampaneze

Lord. Alone they must stand and alone they must succeed or fail."

With that, he brought the meeting to a close. Dismissing Paris and Mika with an arrogant wave of his hand, he beckoned Mr. Crepsley and me forward, and grinned at us as he lay back on my throne. He kicked off one of his boots while he was talking. He wasn't wearing socks, and I was shocked to see he had no toes — his feet were webbed at the ends, with six tiny claws jutting out like a cat's.

"Frightened, Master Shan?" he asked, eyes twinkling mischievously.

"Yes," I said, "but I'm proud to be able to help."

"What if you *aren't* any help?" he jeered. "What if you fail and damn the vampires to extinction?"

I shrugged. "What comes, we take," I said, echoing a saying that was common among the creatures of the night.

Mr. Tiny's smile faded. "I preferred you when you were less clever," he grumbled, then looked to Mr. Crepsley. "What about you? Scared by the weight of your responsibilities?"

"Yes," Mr. Crepsley answered.

"Think you might break beneath it?"

"I might," Mr. Crepsley said evenly.

Mr. Tiny pulled a face. "You two are no fun. It's impossible to get a rise out of you. Harkat!" he bellowed. Harkat approached automatically. "What do you think of this? Does the fate of the vampires bother you?"

"Yes," Harkat replied. "It does."

"You care for them?" Harkat nodded. "Hmmm." Mr. Tiny rubbed his watch, which glowed briefly, then touched the left side of Harkat's head. Harkat gasped and fell to his knees. "You've been having nightmares," Mr. Tiny noted, fingers still at Harkat's temple.

"Yes!" Harkat groaned.

"You want them to stop?"

"Yes."

Mr. Tiny let go of Harkat, who cried out, then gritted his sharp teeth and stood up straight. Small green tears of pain trickled from the corners of his eyes.

"It's time for you to learn the truth about yourself," Mr. Tiny said. "If you come with me, I'll reveal it and the nightmares will stop. If you don't, they'll continue and worsen, and within a year you'll be a screaming wreck."

Harkat trembled at that but didn't rush to Mr. Tiny's side. "If I wait," he said, "will I have . . . another chance to learn . . . the truth?"

"Yes," Mr. Tiny said, "but you'll suffer much in the meantime, and I can't guarantee your safety. If you die before learning who you really are, your soul will be lost forever."

Harkat frowned uncertainly. "I have a feeling," he mumbled. "Something whispers to me —" he touched the left side of his chest "— here. I feel that I should go with Darren . . . and Larten."

"If you do, it will improve their chances of defeating the Vampaneze Lord," Mr. Tiny said. "Your participation isn't instrumental, but it could be important."

"Harkat," I said softly, "you don't owe us. You've already saved my life twice. Go with Mr. Tiny and learn the truth about yourself."

Harkat frowned. "I think that if I . . . leave you to learn the truth, the person I was . . . won't like what I've done." The Little Person spent a few more difficult seconds brooding about it, then squared up to Mr. Tiny. "I'll go with them. Right or wrong, I feel my place is . . . with the vampires. All else must wait."

"So be it," Mr. Tiny sniffed. "If you survive, our paths will cross again. If not . . ." His smile was withering.

"What of our search?" Mr. Crepsley asked. "You mentioned Lady Evanna. Do we start with her?"

"If you wish," Mr. Tiny said. "I can't and won't direct you, but that's where *I* would start. After that, follow your heart. Forget about the quest and go where you feel you belong. Fate will direct you as it pleases."

That was the end of our conversation. Mr. Tiny

slipped away without a farewell, taking his Little People (they completed their repair work while he was talking), no doubt anxious to make it to that fatal volcano of his the next day.

Vampire Mountain was in an uproar that night. Mr. Tiny's visit and prophecy were debated at length. The vampires agreed that Mr. Crepsley and me had to leave on our own, to meet up with the third hunter — whoever he might be — but were divided as to what the rest of them should do. Some thought that since the clan's future rested with three lone hunters, they should forget the war with the vampaneze: It no longer seemed to serve any purpose. Most disagreed and said it would be crazy to stop fighting.

Mr. Crepsley led Harkat and me from the Hall shortly before dawn, leaving the arguing Princes and Generals behind, saying we needed to get a good day's rest. It was hard to sleep with Mr. Tiny's words echoing in my brain, but I managed to squeeze in a few hours.

We woke about three hours before sunset, ate a short meal, and packed our meager belongings (I took a spare set of clothes, some bottles of blood, and my diary). We said private goodbyes to Vanez and Seba — the old quartermaster was especially sad to see us go — then met Paris Skyle at the gate leading out of the Halls. He told us Mika was staying on to assist with the night-to-night running of the war. He looked sick as I shook his hand, and I had a feeling that he didn't have many years left — if our search kept us away from Vampire Mountain for a long period, this might be the last time I saw him.

"I'll miss you, Paris," I said, hugging him roughly after we'd shaken hands.

"I will miss you too, young Prince," he said, then squeezed me tight and hissed in my ear: "Find and kill him, Darren. There is a cold chill in my bones, and it is not the chill of old age. Mr. Tiny has spoken the truth — if the Vampaneze Lord comes into his full powers, I am sure we all shall perish."

"I'll find him," I vowed, locking gazes with the ancient Prince. "And if the chance to kill him falls to me, my aim will be true."

"Then may the luck of the vampires be with you," he said.

I joined Mr. Crepsley and Harkat. We saluted those who'd gathered to see us off, then set off down the tunnels. We moved quickly and surely, and within two hours we had left the mountain and were jogging over open ground, beneath a clear night sky.

Our hunt for the Lord of the Vampaneze had begun!

CHAPTER EIGHT

IT WAS GREAT TO BE BACK on the road. We might be walking into the heart of an inferno, and our companions would suffer immeasurably if we failed, but those were worries for the future. In those first few weeks all I could think about was how refreshing it was to stretch my legs and breathe clean air, not caged in with dozens of sweaty, smelly vampires.

I was in high spirits as we cut a path through the mountains by night. Harkat was very quiet and spent a lot of time thinking about what Mr. Tiny had said. Mr. Crepsley seemed as gloomy as ever, though I knew that underneath the façade he was as pleased to be out in the open as I was.

We kept a steady pace, covering many miles over the course of each night, sleeping deeply by day underneath trees and bushes, or in caves. The cold was fierce when we left, but as we wound our way down the mountain range, the chill lessened. By the time we reached the lowlands we were as comfortable as a human would have been on a blustery autumn day.

We carried spare bottles of human blood and fed on wild animals. It had been a long time since I had hunted, and I was rusty at first, but I soon got back into the swing of it.

"This is the life, isn't it?" I said one morning as we chewed on the roasted carcass of a deer. We didn't light a fire most days — we ate our meat raw — but it was nice to relax around a mound of blazing logs every once in a while.

"It is," Mr. Crepsley agreed.

"I wish we could go on like this forever."

The vampire smiled. "You are not in a hurry to return to Vampire Mountain?"

I pulled a face. "Being a Prince is a great honor, but it's not much fun."

"You have had a rough initiation," he said sympathetically. "Were we not at war, there would have been time for adventure. Most Princes wander the world for decades before settling down to royal duty. Your timing was unfortunate."

"Still, I can't complain," I said cheerfully. "I'm free now."

Harkat stirred up the fire and edged closer toward us. He hadn't said a lot since leaving Vampire Mountain, but now he lowered his mask and spoke. "I loved Vampire Mountain. It felt like home. I never felt so at ease before, even when I . . . was with the Cirque Du Freak. When this is over, if I have . . . the choice, I'll return."

"There is vampire blood in you," Mr. Crepsley said. He was joking, but Harkat took him seriously.

"There might be," he said. "I've often wondered if I was a vampire in . . . my previous life. That might explain why I was sent to Vampire Mountain . . . and why I fitted in so well. It could also explain the stakes . . . in my dreams."

Harkat's dreams often involved stakes. The ground would give way in his nightmares and he'd fall into a pit of stakes, or be chased by shadow men who carried stakes and drove them through his heart.

"Any fresh clues as to who you might have been?" I asked. "Did meeting Mr. Tiny jog your memory?"

Harkat shook his chunky, neckless head. "No further insights," he sighed.

"Why did Mr. Tiny not tell you the truth about yourself if it was time for you to learn?" Mr. Crepsley asked.

"I don't think it's as . . . simple as that," Harkat

said. "I have to earn the truth. It's part of the . . . deal we made."

"Wouldn't it be weird if Harkat *had* been a vampire?" I remarked. "What if he'd been a Prince — would he still be able to open the doors of the Hall of Princes?"

"I don't think I was a Prince." Harkat chuckled, the corners of his wide mouth lifting in a gaping smile.

"Hey," I said, "if *I* can become a Prince, anyone can."

"True," Mr. Crepsley muttered, then ducked swiftly as I tossed a leg of deer at him.

Once clear of the mountains, we headed southeast and soon reached the edge of civilization. It was strange to see electric lights, cars, and planes again. I felt as though I'd been living in the past and had stepped out of a time machine.

"It's so noisy," I commented one night as we passed through a busy town. We'd entered it to draw blood from humans, slicing them in their sleep with our nails, taking a small amount of blood, closing the cuts with Mr. Crepsley's healing spit, and leaving them oblivious to the fact that they'd been fed on. "So much music and laughter and shouting." My ears were ringing from the noise.

"Humans always chatter like monkeys," Mr. Crepsley said. "It is their way."

I used to object when he said things like that, but not any more. When I became Mr. Crepsley's assistant, I'd clung to the hope of returning to my old life. I'd dreamed of regaining my humanity and going home to my family and friends. No longer. My years in Vampire Mountain had rid me of my human desires. I was a creature of the night now — and content to be so.

The itching was getting worse. Before leaving town, I found a pharmacy and bought several anti-itching powders and lotions, which I rubbed into my flesh. The powders and lotions brought no relief. Nothing stopped the itching, and I scratched myself irritably as we journeyed to the cave of Lady Evanna.

Mr. Crepsley wouldn't say much about the woman we were going to meet, where she lived, whether she was a vampire or human, and why we were going to see her.

"You should tell me these things," I grumbled one morning as we made camp. "What if something happens to you? How would Harkat and me find her?"

Mr. Crepsley stroked the long scar running down the left side of his face — after all our years together, I still didn't know how he got it — and nodded thoughtfully. "You are right. I will draw a map before nightfall."

"And tell us who she is?"

He hesitated. "That is harder to explain. It might be best coming from her own lips. Evanna tells different people different things. She might not object to you knowing the truth — but then again, she might."

"Is she an inventor?" I pressed. Mr. Crepsley owned a collection of pots and pans that folded up into tiny bundles, making them easier to carry. He'd told me that Evanna had made them.

"She sometimes invents," he said. "She is a woman of many talents. Much of her time is spent breeding frogs."

I blinked. "Excuse me?" I said.

"It is her hobby. Some people breed horses, dogs, or cats. Evanna breeds frogs."

"How can she breed frogs?" I said with a snort.

"You will find out." Then he leaned forward and tapped my knee. "Whatever you say, do not call her a witch."

"Why would I call her a witch?" I asked.

"Because she is one — sort of."

"We're going to meet a *witch*?" Harkat snapped worriedly.

"That troubles you?" Mr. Crepsley asked.

"Sometimes in my dreams . . . there's a witch. I've never seen her face — not clearly — and I'm not sure . . . if she's good or bad. There are times when I run to her for help, and times . . . when I run away, afraid."

"You haven't mentioned that before," I said.

Harkat's smile was shaky. "With all the dragons, stakes, and shadow men . . . what's one little witch?"

The mention of dragons reminded me of something he'd said when we met Mr. Tiny. He'd called him "the dragon master." I asked Harkat about this but he couldn't remember saying it. "Although," he mused, "I sometimes see Mr. Tiny in my dreams, riding the . . . backs of dragons. Once he tore the brain out of one and . . . tossed it at me. I reached to catch it but . . . woke before I could."

We thought about that image a long time. Vampires place a lot of importance on dreams. Many believe that dreams act as links to the past or future, and that much can be learned from them. But Harkat's dreams didn't seem to have any relation to reality, and in the end Mr. Crepsley and me dismissed them, rolled over, and slept. Harkat didn't — he stayed awake, green eyes glowing faintly, putting off sleep as long as he could, avoiding the dragons, stakes, witches, and other dangers of his nightmares.

CHAPTER NINE

ONE DUSK I AWOKE with a feeling of absolute comfort. As I stared up at a red, darkening sky, I tried to think why I felt so good. Then I realized — the itching had stopped. I lay still a few minutes, afraid it would return if I moved, but when I finally got to my feet, there wasn't the slightest prickling sensation. Grinning, I headed for a small pond we'd camped by, to wet my throat.

I lowered my face into the cool, clear water of the pond and drank deeply. As I was rising, I noticed an unfamiliar face in the reflecting surface of the water — a long-haired, bearded man. It was directly in front of me, which meant he must be standing right behind me — but I hadn't heard anyone approach.

Swiveling swiftly, my hand shot to the sword that

I'd brought from Vampire Mountain. I had it halfway out of its scabbard before stopping, confused.

There was no one there.

I looked around for the shabby, bearded man, but he was nowhere to be seen. There were no nearby trees or rocks he could have ducked behind, and not even a vampire could have moved quickly enough to disappear so swiftly.

I turned back toward the pond and looked into the water again. There he was! As clear and hairy as before, scowling up at me.

I gave a yelp and jumped back from the water's edge. Was the bearded man *in* the pond? If so, how was he breathing?

Stepping forward, I locked gazes with the hairy man — he looked like a caveman — for the third time and smiled. He smiled back. "Hello," I said. His lips moved when mine did, but silently. "My name's Darren Shan." Again his lips moved in time with mine. I was getting annoyed — was he making fun of me? — when the realization struck. It was *me!*

I could see my eyes and the shape of my mouth now that I looked closely, and the small triangular scar just above my right eye, which had become as much a part of me as my nose or ears. It was my face, no doubt about that — but where had all the hair come from?

I felt around my chin and discovered a thick bushy beard. Running my right hand over my head — which should have been smooth — I was stunned to feel long, thick locks of hair. My thumb, which stuck out at an angle, caught in several of the strands, and I winced as I tugged it free, pulling some hair out with it.

What in Khledon Lurt's name had happened to me?

I checked further. Ripping off my T-shirt revealed a chest and stomach covered in hair. Huge balls of hair had also formed under my armpits and over my shoulders. I was hairy all over!

"Charna's guts!" I roared, then ran to wake my friends.

Mr. Crepsley and Harkat were breaking camp when I rushed up, panting and shouting. The vampire took one look at my hairy figure, whipped out a knife, and roared at me to stop. Harkat stepped up beside him, a grim expression on his face. As I halted, gasping for breath, I saw they didn't recognize me. Raising my hands to show they were empty, I croaked, "Don't . . . attack! It's . . . me!"

Mr. Crepsley's eyes widened. *"Darren?"*

"It can't be," Harkat growled. "This is an impostor."

"No!" I moaned. "I woke up, went to the pond to drink, and found . . . found . . ." I shook my hairy arms at them.

Mr. Crepsley stepped forward, sheathed his knife, and studied my face. Then he groaned. "The *purge!*" he muttered.

"The *what?*" I shouted.

"Sit down, Darren," Mr. Crepsley said seriously. "We have a lot of talking to do. Harkat — go fill our canteens and fix a new fire."

When Mr. Crepsley had gathered his thoughts, he explained to Harkat and me what was happening. "You know that half-vampires become full-vampires when more vampire blood is pumped into them. What we have never discussed — since I did not anticipate it so soon — is the other way in which one's blood can turn.

"Basically, if one remains a half-vampire for an extremely long period of time — the average is forty years — one's vampire cells eventually attack the human cells and convert them, resulting in full-vampirism. We call this the purge."

"You mean I've become a full-vampire?" I asked quietly, both excited and frightened at the idea. Excited because it would mean extra strength, the ability to flit and communicate telepathically. Frightened because it would also mean a total retreat from daylight and the world of humanity.

"Not yet," Mr. Crepsley said. "The hair is simply the first stage. We shall shave it off presently, and though it will grow back, it will stop after a month or so. You will undergo other changes during that time — you will grow, and experience headaches and sharp bursts of energy — but these too will cease. At the end of the changes, your vampiric blood may have replaced your human blood entirely, but it probably will not, and you will return to normal — for a few months or a couple of years. But sometime within the next few years, your blood *will* turn completely. You have entered the final stages of half-vampirism. There is no turning back."

We spent most of the rest of the night discussing the purge. Mr. Crepsley said it was rare for a half-vampire to experience the purge after less than twenty years, but it was probably because I'd become a Vampire Prince — more vampiric blood had been added to my veins during the ceremony, and that must have sped up the process.

I remembered Seba studying me in the tunnels of Vampire Mountain, and told Mr. Crepsley about it. "He must have known about the purge," I said. "Why didn't he warn me?"

"It was not his place," Mr. Crepsley said. "As your mentor, I am responsible for informing you. I am sure he would have told me about it, so that I could have sat down with you and explained it, but there was no time — Mr. Tiny arrived and we had to leave the Mountain."

"You said Darren would grow during . . . the purge," Harkat said. "How much?"

"There is no telling," Mr. Crepsley said. "Potentially, he could mature to adulthood in the space of a few months — but that is unlikely. He shall age a few years, but probably no more."

"You mean I'll finally hit my teens?" I asked.

"I would imagine so."

I thought about that for a while, then grinned. "Cool!"

But the purge was far from cool — it was a curse! Shaving off all the hair was bad enough — Mr. Crepsley used a long, sharp blade, which scraped my skin raw — but the changes my body was undergoing were much worse. Bones were lengthening and fusing. My nails and teeth grew — I had to bite my nails and grind my teeth together while I walked at night to keep them in shape — and my feet and hands got longer. Within weeks I was two inches taller, aching all over from growing pains.

My senses were in confusion. Slight sounds were magnified — the snapping of a twig was like a house collapsing. The dullest of smells set my nose tingling. My sense of taste left me completely. Everything tasted like cardboard. I began to understand what life must be like for Harkat and made a resolution never to tease him about his lack of taste buds again.

Even dim lights were blinding to my ultra-sensitive eyes. The moon was like a fierce spotlight in the sky, and if I opened my eyes during the day, I might as well have been sticking two hot pins into them — the inside of my head would flare with a metallic pain.

"Is this what sunlight is like for full-vampires?" I asked Mr. Crepsley one day, as I shivered beneath a thick blanket, eyes shut tight against the painful rays of the sun.

"Yes," he said. "That is why we avoid even short periods of exposure to daylight. The pain of sunburn is not especially great — not for the first ten or fifteen minutes — but the glare of the sun is instantly unbearable."

I suffered immense headaches during the purge, a result of my out-of-control senses. There were times when I thought my head was going to explode, and I'd weep helplessly from the pain.

Mr. Crepsley helped me fight the dizzying effects. He bound light strips of cloth across my eyes — I could still see pretty well — and stuffed balls of grass into my ears and up my nostrils. That was uncomfortable, and I felt ridiculous — Harkat's howls of laughter didn't help — but the headaches lessened.

Another side effect was a fierce surge of energy. I felt as if I were operating on batteries. I had to run ahead of Mr. Crepsley and Harkat at night, then double back to meet them, just to tire myself out. I exercised like crazy every time we stopped — push-ups, pull-ups, sit-ups — and usually woke long before Mr. Crepsley, unable to sleep more than a couple of hours at a time. I climbed trees and cliffs, and swam across rivers and lakes, all in an effort to use up my unnatural store of energy. I'd have wrestled an elephant if I'd found one!

Finally, after six weeks, the turmoil ceased. I stopped growing. I didn't have to shave any more (though the hair on my head remained — I was no longer bald!). I removed the cloth and grass balls, and my taste returned, although patchily to begin with.

I was about three inches taller than I'd been when the purge hit me, and noticeably broader. The skin on my face had hardened, giving me a slightly older appearance — I looked like a fifteen- or sixteen-year-old now.

Most importantly — I was still a half-vampire. The purge hadn't eliminated my human blood cells. The downside was that I'd have to undergo the discomfort of the purge again in the future. On the plus side I could continue to enjoy sunlight for the time being, before having to abandon it forever in favor of the night.

Although I was eager to become a full-vampire, I'd miss the daytime world. Once my blood turned, there was no going back. I accepted that, but I'd be lying if I said I wasn't nervous. This way, I had months — perhaps a year or two — to prepare myself for the change.

I'd outgrown my clothes and shoes, so I had to buy some at a small human outpost (we were leaving civilization behind again). In an army surplus shop, I chose clothing similar to my old stuff, adding a couple of purple shirts to my blue ones, and a dark green pair of pants. As I was paying for the clothes, a tall, lean man entered. He was wearing a brown shirt, black pants, and a baseball cap. "I need supplies," he muttered at the man serving behind the counter, tossing a list at him.

"You'll need a license for the guns," the shopkeeper said, running an eye over the scrap of paper.

"I've got one." The man was reaching into a shirt pocket when he caught sight of my hands and stiffened. I was holding my new clothes across my chest, and the scars on my fingertips — where I'd been blooded by Mr. Crepsley — were clear.

The man relaxed instantly and turned away — but I was sure he'd recognized the scars and knew what I was. Hurrying from the shop, I found Mr. Crepsley and Harkat on the edge of town and told them what had happened.

"Was he nervous?" Mr. Crepsley asked. "Did he follow you when you left?"

"No. He just went stiff when he saw the marks, then acted as though he hadn't seen them. But he knew what the marks meant — I'm sure of it."

Mr. Crepsley rubbed his scar thoughtfully. "Humans who know the truth about vampire marks are uncommon, but some exist. In all probability he is an ordinary person who has simply heard tales of vampires and their fingertips."

"But he *might* be a vampire hunter," I said quietly.

"Vampire hunters are rare — but real." Mr. Crepsley thought it over, then decided. "We will proceed as planned, but keep our eyes open, and you or Harkat will remain on watch by day. If an attack comes, we shall be ready." He smiled tightly and touched the handle of his knife. "And waiting!"

CHAPTER TEN

By DAWN WE KNEW we had a fight on our hands. We were being followed, not just by one person, but three or four. They'd picked up our trail a few miles outside the town and had been tracking us ever since. They moved with admirable stealth, and if we hadn't expected trouble, we might not have known anything was wrong. But when a vampire is alert to danger, not even the fastest human can sneak up on him.

"What's the plan?" Harkat asked as we were making camp in the middle of a small forest, sheltered from the sun beneath the branches and leaves.

"They will wait for full daylight to attack," Mr. Crepsley said, keeping his voice low. "We will act as though all is normal and pretend to sleep. When they come, we deal with them."

"Will you be OK in the sun?" I asked. Though we

were sheltered where we were, a battle might draw us out of the shade.

"The rays will not harm me during the short time it will take to deal with this threat," Mr. Crepsley replied. "And I will protect my eyes with cloth, as you did during your purge."

Making beds in the moss and leaves on the ground, we wrapped ourselves in our cloaks and settled down. "Of course, they might just be curious," Harkat muttered. "They could simply want to see . . . what a real-life vampire looks like."

"They move too keenly for that," Mr. Crepsley disagreed. "They are here on business."

"I just remembered," I hissed. "The guy in the shop was buying *guns!*"

"Most vampire hunters come properly armed," Mr. Crepsley said with a grunt. "Gone are the nights when the fools toted only a hammer and wooden stake."

There was no more talk after that. We lay still, eyes closed (except for Harkat, who covered his lidless eyes with his cloak), breathing evenly, pretending to sleep.

Seconds passed slowly, taking an age to become minutes, and an eternity to become hours. It had been six years since my last taste of vicious combat. My limbs felt unnaturally cold, and stiff, icy snakes of fear coiled and uncoiled inside the walls of my stomach. I kept flexing my fingers beneath the folds of my cloak, never far from my sword, ready to draw.

Shortly after midday — when the sun would be most harmful to a vampire — the humans moved in for the kill. There were three of them, spread out in a semicircle. At first I could hear only the rustling of leaves as they approached, and the occasional snap of a twig. But as they drew closer, I became aware of their heavy breathing, the creak of their tense bones, the panicked pounding of their hearts.

They came to a standstill ten or twelve yards away, tucked behind trees, preparing themselves to attack. There was a long, nervous pause — then the sound of a gun being slowly cocked.

"Now!" Mr. Crepsley roared, springing to his feet, launching himself at the human nearest him.

While Mr. Crepsley closed in on his attacker at incredible speed, Harkat and me targeted the others. The one I'd set my sights on cursed loudly, stepped out from behind his tree, brought his rifle up, and got a snap shot off. A bullet whizzed past, missing me by several inches. Before he could fire again, I was upon him.

I wrenched the rifle from the human's hands and tossed it away. A gun went off behind me, but there was no time to check on my friends. The man in front of me had already drawn a long hunting knife, so I quickly slid my sword out.

The man's eyes widened when he saw the sword — he'd painted the area around his eyes with red circles of what looked like blood — then narrowed. "You're just a kid," he snarled, slashing at me with his knife.

"No," I disagreed, stepping out of range of his knife, jabbing at him with my sword. "I'm much more."

As the human slashed at me again, I brought my sword up and out in a smooth arcing slice, through the flesh, muscles, and bones of his right hand, severing three of his fingers, disarming him in an instant.

The human cried out in agony and fell away from me. I took advantage of the moment to see how Mr. Crepsley and Harkat were doing. Mr. Crepsley had already got rid of his human, and was striding toward Harkat, who was wrestling with his opponent. Harkat appeared to be winning, but Mr. Crepsley was moving into place to back him up should the battle take a turn for the worse.

Satisfied that all was going in our favor, I switched my attention back to the man on the ground, psyching myself up for the unpleasant task of making an end of him. To my surprise, I found him grinning horribly at me.

"You should have taken my other hand too!" he growled.

My eyes fixed on the man's left hand and my breath caught in my throat — he was clutching a hand grenade close to his chest!

"Don't move!" he shouted as I lurched toward him. He half-pressed down on the detonator with his thumb. "If this goes off, it takes you with me!"

"Easy," I said, backing off slightly, gazing fearfully at the primed grenade.

"I'll take it easy in hell." He chuckled sadistically. He'd shaved his head bald and there was a dark "V" tattooed into either side of his skull, just above his ears. "Now, tell your foul vampire partner and that grey-skinned monster to let my companion go, or I'll —"

There was a sharp whistling sound from the trees to my left. Something struck the grenade and sent it flying from the human's hand. He yelled and grabbed for another grenade (he had a string of them strapped around his chest). There was a second whistling sound and a glinting, multi-pointed object buried itself in the middle of the man's head.

The man slumped backward with a grunt, shook crazily, then lay still. I stared at him, bewildered, automatically bending closer for a clearer look. The object in his head was a gold throwing star. Neither Mr. Crepsley nor Harkat carried such a weapon — so who'd thrown it?

In answer to my unvoiced question, someone jumped from a nearby tree and strode toward me. "Only ever turn your back on a corpse!" the stranger snapped as I whirled toward him. "Didn't Vanez Blane teach you that?"

"I . . . forgot," I wheezed, too taken aback to say anything else. The vampire — he had to be one of us — was a burly man of medium height, with reddish skin and dyed green hair, dressed in purple animal skins that had been stitched together crudely. He had huge eyes — almost as large as Harkat's — and a surprisingly small mouth. Unlike Mr. Crepsley, his eyes were uncovered, though he was squinting painfully in the sunlight. He wore no shoes and carried no weapons other than dozens of throwing stars strapped to several belts looped around his torso.

"I'll have my shuriken back, thank you," the vampire said to the dead human, prying the throwing star loose, wiping it clean of blood, and reattaching it to one of the belts. He turned the man's head left and right, taking in the shaved skull, tattoos, and red circles around his eyes. "A vampet!" he snorted. "I've clashed with them before. Miserable curs." He spat on the dead man, then used his bare foot to roll him over, so he was lying face down.

When the vampire turned to address me, I knew who he was — I'd heard him described many times — and greeted him with the respect he deserved. "Vancha March," I said, bowing my head. "It's an honor to meet you, sire."

"Likewise," he replied cheerfully.

Vancha March was the Vampire Prince I'd never met, the wildest and most traditional of all the Princes.

"Vancha!" Mr. Crepsley boomed, tearing the cloth away from around his eyes, crossing the space between us, and clasping the Prince's shoulders. "What are you doing here, sire? I thought you were farther north."

"I was," Vancha sniffed, freeing his hands and wiping the knuckles of his left hand across his nose, then flicking something green and slimy away. "But there was nothing happening, so I cut south. I'm heading for Lady Evanna's."

"We are too," I said.

"I figured as much. I've been trailing you for the last couple of nights."

"You should have introduced yourself sooner, sire," Mr. Crepsley said.

"This is the first time I've seen the new Prince," Vancha replied. "I wanted to observe him from afar for a while." He studied me sternly. "On the basis of this fight, I have to say I'm not overly impressed!"

"I erred, sire," I said stiffly. "I was worried about my friends and I made the mistake of pausing when I should have pushed ahead. I accept full responsibility, and I apologize most humbly."

"At least he knows how to make a good apology," Vancha laughed, clapping me on the back.

Vancha March was covered in grime and dirt and smelled like a wolf. It was his standard appearance. Vancha was a true being of the wilds. Even among vampires, he was considered extreme. He only wore clothes that he'd made himself from wild animal skins, and he never ate cooked meat or drank anything other than fresh water, milk, and blood.

As Harkat limped toward us — having finished off his attacker — Vancha sat and crossed his legs. Lifting his left foot, he lowered his head to it and started biting the nails!

"So this is the Little Person who talks," Vancha mumbled, eyeing Harkat over the nail of his left big toe. "Harkat Mulds, isn't it?"

"It is, sire," Harkat replied, lowering his mask.

"I might as well tell you straight up, Mulds — I don't trust Desmond Tiny or any of his stumpy disciples."

"And I don't trust vampires who . . . chew their toenails," Harkat threw back at him, then paused and added slyly, *"sire."*

Vancha laughed at that and spat out a chunk of nail. "I think we're going to get along fine, Mulds!"

"Hard trek, sire?" Mr. Crepsley asked, sitting down beside the Prince, covering his eyes with cloth again.

"Not bad," Vancha said with a grunt, uncrossing his legs. He then started in on his right toenails. "Yourselves?"

"The traveling has been good."

"Any news from Vampire Mountain?" Vancha asked.

"Lots," Mr. Crepsley said.

"Save it for tonight." Vancha let go of his foot and lay back. He took off his purple cloak and draped it over himself. "Wake me when it's dusk," he yawned, rolled over, fell straight asleep, and started to snore.

I stared, goggle-eyed, at the sleeping Prince, then at the nails he'd chewed off and spat out, then at his ragged clothes and dirty green hair, then at Harkat and Mr. Crepsley. *"He's* a Vampire Prince?" I whispered.

"He is," Mr. Crepsley smiled.

"But he looks like . . ." Harkat muttered uncertainly. "He acts like . . ."

"Do not be fooled by appearances," Mr. Crepsley said. "Vancha chooses to live roughly, but he is the finest of vampires."

"If you say so," I responded doubtfully, and spent most of the day lying on my back, staring up at the cloudy sky, kept awake by the loud snoring of Vancha March.

CHAPTER ELEVEN

WE LEFT THE VAMPETS lying where we'd killed them (Vancha said they weren't worthy of burial) and set off at dusk. As we marched, Mr. Crepsley told the Prince of Mr. Tiny's visit to Vampire Mountain, and what he'd predicted. Vancha said little while Mr. Crepsley was talking, and brooded upon his words in silence for a long time after he finished.

"I don't think it takes a genius to surmise that I'm the third hunter," he said in the end.

"I would be most surprised if you were not," Mr. Crepsley agreed.

Vancha had been picking between his teeth with the tip of a sharp twig. Now he tossed it aside and spat into the dust of the trail. Vancha was a master spitter — his spit was thick, globular, and green, and he could hit an ant at twenty paces. "I don't trust that evil meddler, Tiny," he snapped. "I've run into him a couple of times, and I've made a habit of doing the opposite of anything he says."

Mr. Crepsley nodded. "Generally speaking, I would agree with you. But these are dangerous times, sire, and —"

"Larten!" the Prince interrupted. "It's 'Vancha,' 'March,' or 'Hey, ugly!' while we're on the trail. I won't have you groveling to me."

"Very well —" Mr. Crepsley grinned "— *ugly.*" He grew serious again. "These are dangerous times, Vancha. The future of our race is at stake. Dare we ignore Mr. Tiny's prophecy? If there is hope, we must seize it."

Vancha let out a long, unhappy sigh. "For hundreds of years, Tiny's let us think we were doomed to lose the war when the Vampaneze Lord arose. Why does he tell us now, after all this time, that it *isn't* cut and dried, but we can *only* prevent it if we follow his instructions?" The Prince scratched the back of his neck and spat into the bush to our left. "It sounds like a load of guano to me!"

"Maybe Evanna can shed light on the subject," Mr. Crepsley said. "She shares some of Mr. Tiny's powers and can sense the paths of the future. She might be able to confirm or dismiss his predictions."

"If so, I'll believe her," Vancha said. "Evanna

guards her tongue closely, but when she speaks, she speaks the truth. If she says our destiny lies on the road, I'll gladly tag along with you. If not . . ." He shrugged and let the matter rest.

Vancha March was *weird* — and that was putting it mildly! I'd never met anyone like him. He had a code all of his own. As I already knew, he wouldn't eat cooked meat or drink anything but fresh water, milk, and blood, and he made his clothes from the hides of animals he hunted. But I learned much more about him during the six nights it took us to reach Lady Evanna's.

He followed the old ways of the vampires. Long ago, vampires believed that we were descended from wolves. If we lived good lives and stayed true to our beliefs, we'd become wolves again when we died and roam the wilds of Paradise as spirit creatures of the eternal night. To that end, they lived more like wolves than humans, avoiding civilization except when they had to drink blood, making their own clothes, and following the laws of the wild.

Vancha wouldn't sleep in a coffin — he said they were too comfortable! He thought a vampire should sleep on open ground, covering himself with no more than his cloak. He respected vampires who used coffins but had a very low opinion of those who slept in beds. I didn't dare tell him about my preference for hammocks!

He had a great interest in dreams, and often ate wild mushrooms that led to vibrant dreams and visions. He believed the future was mapped out in our dreams, and if we learned to understand them, we could control our destinies. He was fascinated by Harkat's nightmares and spent many long hours discussing them with the Little Person.

The only weapons he used were his shurikens (the throwing stars), which he carved himself from various metals and stones. He thought hand-to-hand combat should be exactly that — fought with one's hands. He had no use for swords, spears, or axes and refused to touch them.

"But how can you fight someone who has a sword?" I asked one evening as we were getting ready to break camp. "Do you run?"

"I run from nothing!" he replied sharply. "Here — let me show you." Rubbing his hands together, he stood opposite me and told me to draw my sword. When I hesitated, he slapped my left shoulder and jeered. "Afraid?"

"Of course not," I snapped. "I just don't want to hurt you."